# From
# Anne
## to
# Zach

E
MAR

Published by Caroline House
Boyds Mills Press, Inc.
A Highlights Company
815 Church Street
Honesdale, Pennsylvania 18431
Printed in Mexico

Publisher Cataloging-in-Publication Data Martin, Mary Jane.
   From Anne to Zach / by Mary Jane Martin ; illustrated by Michael Grejniec.
—1st ed.
[32]p. : col. ill. ; cm.
Summary : Watercolor illustrations accompany this rhyming alphabet book.
ISBN 1-56397-573-4
1. Children's poetry, American. 2. Alphabet rhymes—Juvenile poetry.
3. Alphabet—Juvenile poetry. [1. American poetry. 2. Alphabet rhymes—Poetry.
3. Alphabet] I. Grejniec, Michael, ill. II. Title
808.81—dc20     1996     AC
Library of Congress Catalog Card Number 95-80227

First edition, 1996
Book designed by Kirchoff/Wohlberg, Inc.
The text of this book is set in 35-point New Windrow Hand Light.
The illustrations are done in watercolors.
Distributed by St. Martin's Press

10 9 8 7 6 5 4 3 2 1

# From Anne to Zach

Mary Jane Martin

illustrations by
Michael Grejniec

Boyds Mills Press

A my name is Anne.

B my name is Barry.

# C my name's Carlotta.

And my dog is hairy.

Very!

D my name is Donna.

E my name is Ed.

# F my name is Frances.

And I stand on my head.

G my name is Ginny.

H my name is Hugh.

I my name's Irene.

# I can jump to 62.

Can you?

J my name is Justin.

K my name is Kate.

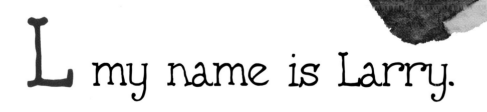

L my name is Larry.

I just learned how to skate.

M my name is Michael.

N my name is Nicki.

O my name is Olaf.

I practice being tricky.

P my name is Paul.

Q my name is Quent.

# R my name is Rhonda.

Once I slept in a tent.

It went!

$\mathcal{S}$ my name is Stephen.

T my name is Tess.

U my name is Uri.
I should clean up this mess.

V my name is Vernon.

W my name is Wynn.

X my name's Xavier.

I can spin and spin and spin.

Y my name is Yetta.
My friends all call me Yet.

Z my name is Zachary.
I can write...

the alphabet.